Curtis is one year, three months and seven days younger than I am, but I don't care. He's the best. He's skinny—not built, like my friend Cluck—but on Curtis, skinny looks great. Anyway, you can tell from his eyes that he's always hearing rock and roll in his head, and his fingers are always sort of strumming the air. Very, very cool.

I've never told anyone this, but I would French kiss Curtis Piperfield if he ever wanted me to. Of course Natalie knows. A best friend just kind of senses when there's someone you want to French kiss, and believe me, I would French kiss Curtis in a hot second. But if the nuns at St. Bernadette's ever heard that, they'd make me say about a billion Hail Marys.

CURTIS PIPERFIELD'S BIGGEST FAN

~~~~~~~~~~~~~~~~~~~~~~~~~~

BY LISA FIEDLER

HarperTrophy®
A Division of HarperCollins*Publishers*

Reprinted by arrangement with Clarion Books,
a Houghton Mifflin Company imprint.
LC Number 95-11702
Trophy ISBN 0-06-440650-4
First Harper Trophy edition, 1997.

This book—every page, every line, every word—is for my mother, the real storyteller in the family, who continues to teach me something every day.

With love to Dad, Ricky, Kiki, Mom, & Dad F.; a big hug for Shannon; and special thanks to Ted, who made it happen.

‗‗‗‗‗‗‗‗‗chapter 1

Curtis Piperfield lives in that house.

That house, right there! Those are his shutters, his porch steps, and that's his bedroom window over there, his *bedroom,* where he keeps his *underwear* and his electric guitar. And where he sleeps, dreaming.

But never of me.

Curtis is going to be a rock star and I am his biggest fan. To the best of my knowledge, I am also his only fan because, at present, Curtis is just an eighth grader at Miltondale Junior High, and eighth graders typically do not generate much of a following.

So, for Curtis Piperfield, eighth grader, one fan is a lot.

I'm in ninth grade, but I don't go to Miltondale.

I go to St. Bernadette's for Girls. It sounds like a reform school, doesn't it? But it's not, it's just Catholic.

Curtis is one year, three months and seven days younger than I am, but I don't care. He's the best. He's skinny—not built, like my friend Cluck—but on Curtis, skinny looks great. He has cinnamon-colored hair and smoldering eyes. I'm not exactly sure if they're gray or hazel because, to be perfectly honest, I haven't gotten many chances to get that close to Curtis. They're sort of *grayzel*, I guess. Anyway, you can tell from his eyes that he's always hearing rock and roll in his head, and his fingers are always sort of strumming the air. Very, very cool.

I've never told anyone this, but I would French kiss Curtis Piperfield if he ever wanted me to. Of course Natalie knows. A best friend just kind of senses when there's someone you want to French kiss, and believe me, I would French kiss Curtis in a hot second. If the nuns at St. Bernadette's ever heard that, they'd make me say about a billion Hail Marys.

My best friend Natalie goes to Miltondale and tells me things I need to know about Curtis. I keep a journal of this information. Natalie thinks nothing of Curtis. She says she never noticed anything special about his eyes, and that *grayzel* is not a word. She says he's a little too young and way too skinny. He is an artist, I am constantly telling her, which cancels out age and weight.

Curtis is the only issue on which Natalie and I do not agree, but I, Cecily Carruthers, am his fan, which is short for fanatic, and that's how I am about Curtis. When he becomes a rock star, this will all pay off.

I'm sitting on the curb waiting for Natalie. I'm looking across the street at Curtis's bedroom window, and I can't help myself, I am thinking I would really like to kiss him. He will get off the bus with Natalie in exactly four-and-a-half minutes and say nothing to me, while I am thinking about kissing him. That, to me, is very hard to accept.

My other best friend, Cluck, shows up. He goes to St. Simon Peter's Boys Prep, and his bus stops here three-and-one-quarter minutes after mine. His uniform tie is the same puke-plaid as my uniform skirt.

"Hi, Cluck."

"Yow! Hi, C.C."

Cluck, unlike Curtis, is close to me a lot, so I know beyond the shadow of a doubt that his eyes

3

are blue, like faded Levi's. Girls always look twice at Cluck, even the seniors, and he says he hates it but I know he's lying. My mother has always said that Gilbert (his real name) is a young Adonis, something I didn't understand until Sister Jude Thaddeus did that unit on mythology.

Cluck runs his hand through his hair, which, it is obvious, has not been brushed today. His hair is silky, brown, and always a little longer than it should be. I am never sure if he forgets to brush it or just refuses to, as a statement. But Cluck would be cute bald, if you want to know the truth.

"I think you need a haircut," I tell him.

Cluck says, "Hair is power, C.C.," whatever that means.

I roll my eyes. "Hair, like power, is a responsibility." This is one of our more philosophical discussions. "You really need a trim."

He drags his hand through his hair again, and there is something masculine and dangerous about the action. But I hardly notice; I've got Curtis on the brain.

"Let's go get some sodas, C.C. I'm thirsty as hell!"

"Don't cuss," I tell him. It's a daily occurrence. "I'm waiting for Nat and the rock star."

Cluck says, "Forget Curtis." Another daily occurrence. Cluck loves me. Always has, always will. But

I wouldn't French kiss him for anything and that kills him.

I let out my breath in one long rush, a sigh which I direct upward to push the bangs off my forehead. This is something I've been doing lately, partly because I'm feeling exasperated a lot, especially when I'm thinking about kissing Curtis and telling Cluck not to cuss, and partly because I'm only three days into this haircut, and I'm not used to the bangs.

Neither is Cluck. "Why'd you get your damn hair cut anyway?"

"To bother you."

Cluck gives me this look that is a cross between heartbreak and fury. "I loved your hair. Man, I *loved* it."

So did I. My hair is strawberry-blond, and until three days ago it was long, about halfway down my back. I got it cut in a moment of vanity overload, when the stylist at the hair-cutting place told me I'd look much older, not to mention more glamorous, with it short.

"I should have saved you what was cut off," I joke, but Cluck loves me so much, I think he wishes I had.

Then the Miltondale bus chugs to a stop and Curtis Piperfield, in excellent blue jeans, hops off.

Someday I am going to kidnap him. But not today.

Curtis says hi to Cluck and keeps going. Then Natalie appears.

Natalie is wearing an outfit I've never seen before: a very cool shirt and jeans. Today she looks modern, but with Nat you never know. Tomorrow she might go totally retro. It's hard to keep up. Her hair is also different every day. It's shoulder-length and–she says–dirty-blonde. She's been begging her mom to let her get highlights. But so far, it's been no-go on the dye job, so Natalie compensates by buying tons of clothes. She has the best clothes you've ever seen, and I hate standing next to her in my St. Bernie's stuff.

"You're not going to like this, C.C.," she says.

"Tell me."

"Curtis likes Bridget Glenn."

"Liar."

"I'm not. He told me he likes Bridget Glenn."

Cluck has removed his tie and is whirling it above his head like a lariat. "Everybody likes Bridget Glenn," he says and licks his lips. "'Cept me."

"Bridget Glenn?" I yell. "She's as dumb as a dead monkey and about as pretty!"

"Now who's a liar?" Natalie says.

She's right. Bridget Glenn bears no resemblance whatsoever to a monkey, dead or alive. Bridget

Glenn looks like a movie star. At the moment, she is a seventh grader at Miltondale Junior High, but someday she'll be Miss America.

"What's so great about Bridget Glenn?" I want to know.

"She's got big breasts!" Cluck tells me.

"So what? What good are breasts to a seventh grader?" It's a stupid thing to say, but I say it anyway.

"Plenty good!" Cluck reports, and Natalie kicks him in the shin.

I can't believe someone as artistic as Curtis Piperfield, the most talented eighth-grade guitar player in Miltondale and quite possibly the United States of America, could like someone based on the size of her chest. But Natalie swears on my St. Bernie's history book (which I figure is an adequate substitute for the Holy Bible) that Curtis likes Bridget.

Curtis, with his smoldering eyes.

Curtis, the boy I've been wanting to French kiss.

Curtis, Curtis, Curtis! Curtis Piperfield who is going to be a rock star likes Bridget and not me.

I turn my face so Cluck and Nat won't notice I'm on the verge of crying, and we head to the burger place for sodas.

chapter 2 ──────────

I discovered Curtis two hours after he moved in across the street. He was in fifth grade at the time, I was in sixth, and he was carrying a hamster cage into his house.

I liked him then and there.

The next day I took Curtis some hamster food in a Tupperware bowl with a lid on it, which my mother made me promise to bring back. The food was left over from when I brought the sixth grade's hamster home for Christmas break, almost five months before. I hoped it hadn't gone bad or turned sour or whatever happens to old hamster food, because killing a kid's hamster isn't exactly the best way to get him to like you.

I knocked on the door. I was excited—a little

worried about the possibility of having a dead hamster on my conscience, but mostly excited.

Curtis opened the door, and I said, "Hello."

"Hi," he said. "What's in the bowl?"

I shook it around. It made an interesting noise. "Hamster food. Welcome to the neighborhood. I'm Cecily Carruthers and I live there." I jerked my thumb in the direction of my house. "What's your name?"

"Curtis."

That's when Cluck rode by on his bike and skidded to a halt. He didn't like me talking to boys other than him because, as I have said, Cluck has always loved me. "Hey, who's the new kid?" he yelled, letting his bicycle clatter to the sidewalk.

"Curtis!" I said, wishing Cluck would vanish, at least for the afternoon.

"Yow, Curtis!" (Which meant, "Nice to meet you, let's be friends, where's your bike?" in Cluck.)

Curtis seemed a lot happier to see Cluck than me, and it warmed him enough to get us invited inside. He'd probably only meant for Cluck to come in, but I was the one with the hamster food, so I went in anyway.

We followed Curtis through the house. "My room," he announced. "My hamster."

I was liking Curtis so much that I didn't even mind that he and Cluck ignored me the entire three hours we spent there. I held the Tupperware bowl the whole time and never bothered to feed the hamster.

That was the day Curtis told us he was going to learn guitar and be a rock star, and I decided to be his first fan. Curtis and Cluck wound up being pretty good pals all through grammar school. Curtis and I wound up being nothing.

Back then, Curtis went to Thomas Jefferson Elementary and Cluck and I went to Central Catholic Grammar. When our school let out early on Holy Days of Obligation, we would wait on the Thomas Jefferson playground for Curtis to get out of school, and we'd all walk home together. It was always pretty much the way it had been that first day in Curtis's bedroom, except without the hamster food. Cluck ignored me, but he loved me. Curtis just ignored me.

That first night, when he told us he was going to be a rock star and I decided to be his biggest fan, I made the first entry in my Curtis journal:

You never thanked me for the hamster food. But when you become a rock star and your father lets you pierce your ear and stay up past ten o'clock on school nights, you and I will be perfect together.

The burger place is jammed. Natalie orders a diet root beer and Cluck and I ask for Cokes. We get a booth and it takes about two hundred years for our sodas to come. I'm still not happy about the news Natalie's given me.

"Let's see a movie tonight," Cluck suggests. He does this every Thursday. He makes it sound as if he's inviting Natalie and me, but we both know this is Cluck's way of asking me on a date. It almost worked once; then after we said we'd go, he took Natalie aside and offered her nine dollars to back out. Cluck's our best friend but he can be a real jerk sometimes.

"No!" we say.

Cluck sees Walter Mert and Frankie Bruno and he goes over to talk to them for a few minutes. They're both cute, but neither of them is as spectacular as Cluck. And besides, I'm Curtis Piperfield's biggest fan.

"The trouble with you and Curtis," Natalie is explaining to me, "is that you don't communicate."

For somebody who drinks diet root beer, Natalie can be pretty insightful.

■

I decide that writing Curtis a note is my best

bet. Not a love note; that would be dumb. Definitely not a Do-You-Like-Me? note either, because I am painfully aware of what the answer would be. Instead, I decide to appeal to his desire for stardom and focus on his becoming a rock and roll idol.

The note is a list of possible names for Curtis Piperfield's band. *Dirt Rainbow* is one. *Straitjacket, Plastic Skuz.* Natalie likes *Uncle Switchblade* and Cluck thinks the whole idea is stupid.

"Forget Curtis," he says.

Morning Breath. Stiff Planet. Hamster Food. I slip that in as a hint, but I don't sign my name. I give the note to Natalie to give to Curtis.

Natalie is impressed. "C.C." she says, tucking the note into her book bag, "you are far too sophisticated and much too good looking to be stuck at St. Bernadette's for Girls."

It would be conceited to agree with her, but deep down, I think she's right.

Once, Cluck told me that the boys at Simon Pete's talk about me in gym class and sometimes even in chapel, which, if they're saying what I think they're saying, could get them all shot straight to hell. There are a few boys at Simon Pete's that I'm glad to have talking about me and even a few

I think I might like to kiss you-know-how, although none as much as you-know-who. Natalie says I think about kissing way too much, but when you're surrounded by nuns all day, there's not much else to consider.

chapter 3 ～～～～～～～～

The closest thing I have to a best friend at St. Bernie's is Grace Boccaluzzo. I can't call her a real best friend because I've only known her since the beginning of ninth grade, unlike Nat and Cluck, whom I've known practically since birth. I am of the opinion that you need to know someone longer than seven months to consider her a best friend. For example, Grace still hasn't figured out that I want to French kiss Curtis Piperfield.

Grace Boccaluzzo and I have almost every class together, including morality with Sister Edward, who is going to be six hundred this year and has been wearing the same shoes since 1972.

Today in class we are discussing Sister Ed's favorite subject: premarital sex. She has one opinion on the topic, which should be pretty easy to guess, and in class we all agree with her one hundred percent.

Grace has just slipped me a note. It says the same thing it always says: "This class is soooooooooo boring!" If there is ever a shortage of *o*'s in this country, it will be Grace Boccaluzzo's fault.

I write back: "Sister Ed is a beast!" Then I cross out the *S* in Sister and change it to "*M*ister Ed"—an old joke, but it's difficult to be creative when a six-hundred-year-old nun is discussing abstinence. I slip it back to Grace who writes: "Yeah." Then she doodles one of her famous "Grace luvs Cluck" masterpieces. I hate "luvs." I have this urge to correct it, but she'd just use it again in the next note, I'm sure. Grace has no respect for the alphabet.

Mister Ed, the talking nun, is defining chastity. Oh, Wilbur! I write back to Grace: "I'm calling Cluck from the lunchroom at 12:07," and at this, Grace nearly begins to sweat. She loves Cluck the way I love Curtis, and she can't wait for me to call him. She'll even supply the change.

Mister Ed is looking for victims. "Miss Boccaluzzo," she booms.

Grace crumples the note and looks up, terrified. "Yes, Sister?"

"Miss Boccaluzzo, recite for us please the cardinal sins." The way she's glaring at the scrap of loose-leaf paper in Grace's hand, you'd think passing notes was one of them.

"Um. Well. There's, um . . ."

I don't know them either, except for gluttony and the only reason I remember that one is because morality comes right before lunch. When it is evident that Grace does not know the answer, Mister Ed says, "Anyone?" and of course, Kelly Sinclair raises her hand.

"Yes, Miss Sinclair?"

"Pride, lust, envy, anger, covetousness, gluttony, and sloth."

"Excellent."

Kelly Sinclair, if you want to get an idea of what type she is, wore lip gloss in fourth grade and got away with it. And beneath her picture in the Central Catholic eighth-grade yearbook, it said, "Sugar and spice and everything nice. God's Favorite Cheerleader." She was actually thrilled about that. Kelly was also voted Class Flirt, but she only came in second for Best Looking. Guess who came in first. Me. That knocked Kelly right out of her saddle shoes.

"Gilbert is sooooooo handsome," Grace tells me as we are walking to the lunchroom.

"Gilbert likes to be called Cluck," I inform her for the billionth time, but I'm dreading the day she asks me where that nickname came from, because I don't know. We've called him that since second grade, and I've always wondered why. I actually asked him a couple of times. He turned red and refused to enlighten me, so I figured it must be some disgusting boy thing. However, since I sort of like being St. Bernie's foremost authority on Gilbert "Cluck" McNally, I really don't want Grace to know that I don't know.

"All the girls at St. Bernie's like Gilbert," Grace is telling me. "Even Kelly Sinclair. He's delicious."

Now, why would anyone describe a boy—especially Cluck—as delicious?

This is why all-girls schools are such a bad idea. All day long we're penned up hearing about sins of the flesh and impure thoughts. Then they let us out, and there go the hormonal floodgates, so that all it takes is one boy in a Simon Pete's blazer and puke-plaid tie to destroy an entire semester's worth of morality, catechism, and advanced placement religious theory. Personally, if Mister Ed ever so much as mentions French kissing in class, I think I will grab Curtis Piperfield the minute he gets off the Miltondale Junior High School bus and . . . well, you know.

"Cluck is no Curtis Piperfield, that's for sure," I tell Grace.

"Gilbert is much more attractive than Curtis," Grace counters. "Curtis is an eighth grader. He hasn't matured yet. Gilbert, on the other hand, is de-lish!"

Why argue? And besides, if I weren't so sure that Curtis was going to be a rock star, I might be satisfied with Cluck. But when I hear Curtis on his electric guitar, I just get crazy, which is why I am such a natural at being a fan.

■

The only thing that distinguishes St. Bernadette's for Girls from a maximum-security prison is the pay telephone in the lunchroom. The same is true of St. Simon Peter's, so every day at 12:07 I can call Cluck.

"Yow!" He answers. "Hi, C.C. How's my girl?"

"Hi, Cluck. I'm not your girl. What's for lunch there?"

"Macaroni and cheese. How about there?"

"Fish sticks and creamed corn. Is anyone talking about me?"

Cluck seems reluctant to tell. He finally admits that Patrick O'Connell prayed for me in chapel.

This is flattering but strange. "Does Patrick O'Connell know something I don't?"

Cluck explains that the prayer was purely preventative. Patrick is just worried something terrible could happen to me before he ever gets a chance to know me in the biblical sense.

Patrick O'Connell is one of the boys I'd like to French kiss one day. He's what my mother would call an all-American boy, which in her hierarchy is second only to a young Adonis. Patrick has hair about the same color as Natalie's. Not too blond. Just blond enough. He's got very sexy green eyes and a sexy smile to go with them. I've given a lot of thought to Patrick over the years, but I don't like the fact that he is planning to engage in premarital relations with me. If Sister Edward heard this, she'd hemorrhage.

"Tell Patrick to cut that out," I say and then, because Grace is practically jumping up and down, I add, "Grace Boccaluzzo says hi."

"Who?"

"Cluck says hi," I tell Grace, and her day is made. "What's for dessert, Cluck?"

"The usual, yellow Jell-O."

Cluck has to go or he'll miss the macaroni and cheese, so I say, "See ya."

And Cluck says, "Bye, babe," which I hate.

chapter 4 ~~~~~~~~~~~~~~~~~

Sister Jude Thaddeus is the scariest nun at St. Bernadette's.

Not scary like ugly—in fact, she's actually kind of pretty. And not scary like mean, either. Sister Jude doesn't scream and she doesn't try to intimidate you. She's basically nice. What *is* scary about her is that you always get the feeling she can see straight through your skin, straight through your eyeballs, and she knows what you're thinking. She teaches English, and for a nun she's a pretty creative type. She even tried to start up an elective course called "Intro to Film as a Genre." Nobody was surprised when the class wasn't approved because, seriously, have you ever seen nuns go to the movies?

Sister Jude was the one who did the unit on

mythology. I give her a lot of credit because mythology has a fair amount of sex in it, especially where Zeus is concerned, but she went right ahead and taught it anyway. Then she got us started on poetry, which I really liked. I'm a word person, like Curtis is a music person and Natalie is a clothes person. "Grayzel," for example, makes perfect sense to me. But I didn't know this was a prerequisite to writing poetry.

Last week, Sister Jude closed her unit on poetry by assigning an original poem. "Any length, any style, any subject," she said. "As long as it's your own creation, you can write in any form and on any topic you wish." Along with being a borderline psychic, Sister Jude is a liberal.

That night Cluck and I did our homework together at my kitchen table.

Cluck is a math person, but you'd never know it to listen to him complain. He slid his book across the table, and it almost knocked over my Coke. "I hate this damn algebra."

"Don't cuss, Cluck."

"What the hell good is algebra?"

"Cluck!"

He stood up and opened the refrigerator. He closed it. He went to the sink and turned on the water. When Cluck gets antsy, there's no stopping him.

I told him to cut it out, I was working.

He told me he thought I had the most gorgeous neck he'd ever seen, he wanted to kiss it . . . No way, Cluck . . . One little kiss? . . . Cluck, you know better . . . C.C., you do something to me. The usual dialogue.

"Will you please finish your algebra so I can concentrate?"

Cluck sat back down and shut up for about forty-five minutes. So for forty-five minutes, I worked on my poem which—big surprise—happened to be about Curtis Piperfield.

"C.C.? Hey, C.C.," Cluck was saying.

I looked up from the page, and I had this ridiculous feeling that I was naked, which of course, I wasn't.

"I've got to go," Cluck said.

"Oh. Okay. Thanks for being quiet."

"I was watching you."

"Watching me what?"

"Just watching you."

"Go home, Cluck."

"I'm going." Cluck picked up his books. Before he left the kitchen he whispered, "Bye, babe."

I *hate* that.

Sister Jude sends Mary Margaret Hennessy to get me from the lunchroom; Mary Margaret finds me at the pay phone just as I am hanging up on Cluck. Fine with me. I'm not exactly crazy about fish sticks anyway. When I walk into Sister Jude's classroom, she is sitting at her desk holding a piece of notebook paper, which I recognize right away as the original poem I handed in on Tuesday. She turns in her chair to see through me better and says, "I'd like to talk to you about your poem, C.C."

Another scary thing about Sister Jude is that she's the only nun who calls me C.C. At St. Bernadette's, you're Kathleen, not Kate; you're Elizabeth, not Liz. Even Mary Margaret Hennessy isn't just plain Mary, and you'd think they'd call girls Mary every chance they got. All the other nuns call me Cecily or Miss Carruthers, which in my opinion is a stupid thing to call a fourteen-year-old. Sister Jude calls me C.C. I don't know why I find this spooky, but I do.

She's reading the poem to herself and I'm thinking: Here it comes. I knew she was going to hate it. I knew, because the poem is extremely sexy. She's creative, but let's face it, she's a nun and sexy poems are probably not her favorite type. I don't even know where I got the nerve to hand it in.

"It's wonderful, C.C. Outstanding. Have you written poetry before?"

She's kidding, right? *Outstanding?* I shrug. "Um. Nope. I mean, no. Not exactly. I keep a journal. You might say it's poetic. Sort of." I am referring to the journal I keep about Curtis.

Sister taps the notebook paper with her finger. "This is an excellent first attempt. Very expressive."

Any minute now, she's going to send me to detention, possibly with a detour to the confessional, for writing such a sexy poem. She's just being polite and saying *expressive* instead of *sexy.* This is a good thing, because if I ever heard a nun use the word "sexy" I'd probably go into shock.

"Oh. Well. Thank you." What am I supposed to say?

"Unfortunately, we've completed our unit on poetry."

I nod, as if this depresses me a lot.

"But I don't think you should give up writing. Would you like to pursue your writing, C.C.?"

Pursue my writing. I don't know. I don't answer her.

"Well, I'd be happy to read anything you write and discuss it with you."

"That'd be great. Really. Thanks." The weird thing is, I'm beginning to think I *could* write some more. And I'm starting to believe, from the way Sister Jude is grinning, that maybe it wasn't a bad poem at that. I remember how I felt when I wrote it—lost, kind of goosebumpy, naked. And, as I mentioned, I was sitting at the kitchen table with Cluck at the time and was most definitely not naked. But I felt like I was, which is what's making me think it's a pretty good poem.

Now she isn't saying anything so I stumble on. "Thanks. If I write any more poems . . . I mean, if I have the time . . . yeah, sure. You can read them. But I'm not sure I'll have time because I've been having trouble with morality—the class, I mean—because there's so much reading—and I'm not exactly a whiz at algebra either. But if I get a chance, you know, if I have the time . . . sure."

She smiles and hands me the poem. "Find time. I think you've got talent."

"Thanks," I say, for what seems like the zillionth time. And I leave.

All the way to my locker and then all the way to physical science, I think about my poem, and the whole time Sister Catherine is handing out beakers, I'm still thinking about it.

The truth is, I want to write more poetry. But what I don't want to do is spend one fraction of a second longer than I have to with an English teacher who also happens to be a nun with the ability to see into your head.

Sister Catherine summarizes today's experiment; I read my poem:

PERFORMANCE

His music is full of silence and love
　　　whispers in.
Pink light in pools, like wounds
　　　on a blue stage
Where I surround his sadness,
Cradling the music in my hands.
And I, the trembling dancer,
Finish soft upon his lips.
I spill away from him
Like a song.

~~~~~~~~~~~~~~~~chapter 5

Curtis read my note once, crumpled it, and tossed it across study hall into the wastebasket, that's what Natalie tells me and Cluck on Saturday.

"Did he even grin?" I want to know. "Did he ask who sent it?"

Natalie says no and this leaves me feeling empty.

"Personally," I tell them, "I think *Straitjacket* is a good name for a band."

"If you keep chasing after Curtis, you're going to end up in one," Cluck says.

"A band?"

"A straitjacket, C.C. Forget Curtis."

Cluck is nuts about me, poor kid.

We're waiting for Grace Boccaluzzo, who is in the drugstore buying tampons, something I wouldn't do within a thirty-mile radius of a boy from St. Simon Peter's Prep, especially one that I like as much as Grace likes Cluck. But Grace made it abundantly clear to us what she was going into Durgan's Pharmacy to purchase. I suppose she wants to establish herself as a woman in Cluck's eyes. Should I mention to her that it probably won't make any difference to Cluck, considering he's loved me since before I was old enough to spit, let alone menstruate?

Grace comes out and we walk for a while. Natalie is talking about which dress she's going to lend me for the spring formal, which is two weeks from today. The spring formal is really just a mixer in the St. Bernadette's gym, but it's the one occasion of the year when the Bernie Girls are actually encouraged to mingle with the Preppies from Simon Pete's.

"Who are you going to ask, Gilbert?" Grace wants to know.

Grace is looking at him and he is looking at me and I am looking at Natalie (who is looking at dresses in Braddock's window) because I know that Cluck is going to ask me.

Then Cluck says something that shocks all of us: "Kelly Sinclair."

And Natalie isn't looking at dresses anymore. Probably because absolutely nothing in Braddock's window can compare with the look on my face.

After me, Kelly Sinclair is the Bernie girl the Simon Pete's boys think about most. She's an idiot and I can't believe Cluck has even the remotest inclination to take her to the formal. But I'm not going to say anything, because it would sound as if I cared or was jealous.

Grace, on the other hand, says plenty. "Kelly Sinclair? You're kidding! Why?"

"Because she's a nymphet."

I have *never* heard Cluck use that word before. Neither has Natalie. "What's *that*?"

Cluck thinks before he answers. "A girl I would like to kiss."

I am no nymphet! What is he talking about?

"You would like to kiss Kelly Sinclair?" Grace asks.

Cluck smiles. "In various places." Cluck can be sick sometimes.

I think I remember something about nymphets from Sister Jude's mythology lessons. Or maybe it was wood nymphs. "Where did you learn that word?" I ask.

"Salvatore Malanconico looked it up."

"I didn't know Salvatore had such a thirst for knowledge." I am being very sarcastic.

Grace looks sullen. "So what does it mean?"

"It means a sexually attractive young girl." Cluck smiles again.

Now, I am all for Cluck expanding his vocabulary, with or without the assistance of Sal Malanconico, but I doubt very much that the word *nymphet* is going to appear on the PSATs. Natalie goes back to looking in Braddock's window. Grace looks as if she might cry.

We dump Cluck at the junior high, where he is meeting Walter Mert for basketball. Today I am glad to be rid of him; that comment about wanting to kiss a nymphet left me clammy.

"I was hoping he'd ask me," Grace says, when Cluck is dribbling with Walter.

It had never once crossed my mind that Cluck would ask somebody other than me. He'd ask me, I'd turn him down, and he would go with Walter Mert and Frankie Bruno and stand against the bleachers staring at me all night.

Kelly Sinclair would accept Cluck's invitation, naturally, because she, like Grace, thinks that Cluck is delicious. This does not bother me exactly, but it does itch a little at the back of my brain, the way a scratchy collar tag itches the back of your neck.

I say, "I am taking Curtis Piperfield."

Natalie bets me a zillion dollars he will not accept.

Grace says she'll settle for Russell Blake, who sent her a valentine last February. He is a ninth grader at Miltondale and they had the same orthodontist.

That, I say to myself, is the basis of a lasting relationship.

We stop at the burger place for sodas. Before the night is over, I decide, I am going to ask Curtis Piperfield to the spring formal.

chapter 6 ~~~~~~~~~~~~~~~~

When I get home, I make an entry in my Curtis journal:

I hope you know that it has not been easy for me. I've believed in you since the minute you said you were going to be a rock star, and sometimes I think the second I stop loving you, I'll disappear. Or explode.

Then I write Cluck's definition of *nymphet*. I don't think I'll ever have cause to use it in a sentence, certainly not in conversation—possibly in a poem, but even that is not likely. And then, because I don't have all that much confidence in Sal Malanconico's verbal skills, I look it up myself and the word immediately following *nymphet* catches my attention—it's *nymphomania,* meaning excessive sexual desire in a female.

I slam the dictionary shut and put my journal

back in its hiding place. Then I go down the hall to the family room where my mother is cutting Easter lilies out of construction paper. My mother is a kindergarten teacher at Central Catholic; this is her first year. She used to teach in the public school.

"Hi, sweetheart."

"Hi, Mom."

She holds up a white lily and asks me how I like it. "I love it," I tell her. "Best paper lily I've ever seen." I manage to make this sound sincere.

"It's for my bulletin board." She uses a glue stick to secure the lily to a green construction-paper stem. "It's nice to be able to do an Easter theme instead of the nondenominational ones I did at Jefferson."

Mom takes her bulletin boards very seriously.

I offer to help her cut out eggs and bunnies. "The spring formal's coming up," I tell her.

"I know." She gives me a big smile. "Has Gilbert asked you yet?"

There's a strange, sinking feeling in my stomach when I tell her he's going to ask Kelly. I leave out the nymphet part. "Anyway," I say, "I don't want to go with Cluck. I want to go with Curtis."

Mom looks at me as if I'd just told her I wanted to go to the spring formal with Judas Iscariot and that I needed thirty pieces of silver for a new dress. "Curtis? Curtis across the street?" That's what she calls him, Curtis-Across-the-Street.

"Yes," I say. "He's cute. And he plays the guitar."

Mom is cutting out letters to spell Hallelujah. "Have you asked him yet?"

"Not yet. I'm going over there right before dinner."

Mom leans over and kisses me on top of my head. Then she hands me the scissors, and I finish up the letters for her. But my mind is not on spelling. My mind is on Curtis.

What else is new?

■

I knock on the Piperfield's front door. Curtis's little sister Meredith answers.

"Hi there, Cecily Carruthers."

"Is Curtis home?"

"No, he's not here."

"Well, can I come in?" I'm not sure why I ask. Curtis isn't home, but I feel this urge to be in his house.

"If you want." She steps aside. I am in Curtis's house.

When Mrs. Piperfield appears and asks if there

is something she can do for me, I lie. "I left something here and I came to get it."

You would think Mrs. Piperfield would know this is a fib because I have not set foot in her house since the day I brought Curtis hamster food, three years ago.

But Mrs. Piperfield just smiles and says, "Oh? What?"

"A Tupperware bowl. With a lid."

I tell her I probably left it in Curtis's room and she tells me I can go get it; she's got a soufflé in the oven which requires constant supervision.

Curtis's room is down the hall and I head there. It's weird and familiar because all of the houses in our neighborhood have the same floor plan—they're ranch-style—and Curtis's room in his house is in the same place as my room in my house. I've always thought this implied some kind of cosmic connection between us.

When I reach Curtis's door, I am suddenly aware of every nerve ending in my body; I feel sort of the way I did when I wrote the poem about him, all goosebumpy and light-headed. I turn the doorknob, enter the room, and immediately, I am happier than I have ever been in my life.

I am standing in Curtis Piperfield's bedroom!

It is nothing like the first time, because Cluck

isn't here, which makes it a lot more intimate. Of course, Curtis isn't here either. But his *stuff* is. His electric guitar is leaning in the corner. His homework is half finished on his desk. His sneakers are sticking out from under his bed . . . Curtis Piperfield's *bed*!

Very quietly, I move toward it. It has not been made. The sheets are rumpled and the quilt is on the floor. I want to bury my face in his pillow and breathe him in. I sit down and the next thing I know, I am lying on Curtis's bed, wondering: Curtis Piperfield, have you ever been French kissed?

We haven't covered this in morality, but I'm pretty certain it is a flat-out sin. A couple of Hail Marys will probably fix me; it's not as if Curtis were *in* his bed at the moment. (I am lying on Curtis's bed and I am thinking about penance, which should be an indication of how Catholic school can really ruin you.)

I get up and notice he's got junk on his dresser: a comb, some pennies, a pack of gum, and a note. The note is written in pink ink on pink stationery, which worries me because this level of cuteness could only be achieved by the public-school equivalent of Kelly Sinclair, who just happens to be

Bridget Glenn. Sure enough, I pick up the note and the outside says, *To: Curtis, From: Bridget.*

I am thoroughly disgusted to discover that Bridget dots her *i*'s with little hearts; there's a big fat one over the *i* in Curtis and a little dainty one over the *i* in Bridget. I can't help myself. I open the note.

Oh God, it's one of *those*! One of those pass-back-and-forth-in-class notes! Curtis's crummy penmanship and Bridget's ridiculous heart-dotted-*i*-writing on the same piece of paper is almost too much to bear.

Bridget wrote first: "Study hall is a bore!"

Curtis wrote: "Yeah."

My stomach is in knots and I might vomit. Bridget's exclamation points have little smiley faces at the bottom. I hate her. Her and her smiley faces and her little hearts and her breasts.

Bridget wrote: "Curtis, I know someone who likes you."

Curtis responds: "Who?"

Bridget thinks she's so clever, she writes: "Guess! She's in this room and she's got blond hair."

Curtis, my future rock star, writes: "I know who I *hope* it is."

"Who?" writes Bridget.

At this point, I wish I could die because, naturally, Curtis has written: "You."

And Bridget Glenn responds with: "I like you, too."

And then—*and then*—Curtis Piperfield, the world's greatest skinny, smoldery-eyed, eighth-grade guitar player, actually *doodles,* in the tradition of Grace Boccaluzzo, a cockeyed heart with "Curtis + Bridget" inside.

Suddenly I'm as desperate to get out this room as I was to get into it. But when I turn around I see Curtis Piperfield in the doorway, and—you can't blame him—he wants to know what the hell I'm doing.

What the hell *am* I doing?

chapter 7

I'm still holding the note in my hand. "Curtis," I say, "would you like to go to the St. Bernadette's Spring Formal with me?"

"What the hell are you doing?" Curtis says again.

It is as if everything in the room—the guitar, the pillow, his sneakers—has leaned in to listen to us. I feel squashed and out of place, but mostly I feel this incredible urge to kiss him.

I put down Bridget's little hearts and smiley faces. "Would you?"

Curtis is glaring at me. It must seem like a stupid question to him, since he's just caught me snooping through his bedroom. I guess it would have made more sense if I'd said, "Curtis, would you like to call the police?"

Now, it is pretty clear to me that Curtis does *not* want to go to the spring formal with me, and I feel this weird, horrible tightening in my heart because I realize that I've just blown any chance I ever had with him.

So I say, "Never mind, Curtis, forget it," and although I fully intend to make my exit at this point, the next thing I know, my arms are around him and my body is pressed against his and *I am kissing Curtis Piperfield!*

When I finally make myself stop, Curtis says the third thing he's said to me today, which happens to be the same as the first two things: "What the hell are you doing?"

I don't answer him. I leave. Just like that. I leave. At least now I am completely certain of one very important thing, and that is: *Yes, Curtis Piperfield definitely has been French kissed.*

■

I call Natalie the second I get in the front door, and it is not until the fourth ring that I notice the phone cord is bouncing around like crazy. Then I realize this is because my hands are shaking. Also my knees are shaking. And several of my internal organs are shaking, too. Let me tell you, when your liver is shaking, you don't feel as if you've just French kissed a future rock star. You feel as if you're going to throw up.

"Hello?"

"I did it," I tell her. And this is how I know Natalie is my best friend for life: She knows exactly what I'm talking about.

"When?"

"Just now, in his bedroom."

"Mother of God! How many Hail Marys do you think that'll cost you?"

I can't guess. I don't care. I am wondering if Curtis is going to write this in his next note to Bridget Glenn.

Natalie says, "Don't move, I'll be right over."

■

Nat arrives at my front door with a sleeping bag and a double batch of chocolate chip cookies. Apparently, while I was attacking Curtis, Nat was dropping dough by rounded teaspoonfuls onto an ungreased cookie sheet. I am very happy to see the cookies. Kissing made me hungry.

"Mother of God!" Natalie says again. For a Protestant, she says that kind of stuff a lot.

We go directly to my room. First she wants to

know what Curtis was wearing. Then I tell her exactly what happened and try my best to describe the smell of Curtis's pillow: "Sweet, a little like sweat, a little like skin, but dustier."

Natalie is not especially interested in the bedding; she wants to know about the kiss. "Do you think he enjoyed it?"

I am on my fifth cookie. "Hard to say," I admit. "There was a lot of saliva involved, and I might have bitten him by accident." I have already decided that if Curtis ever approaches me on the biting part, I will say I did it on purpose, that it's just the way I kiss. Natalie thinks this is probably my best bet. I wonder if Curtis's lip is swelling.

"What about the formal, C.C.? Did he say he would go?"

"He didn't say he wouldn't."

"That's close."

Not close enough, I am thinking. He likes Bridget, as Natalie already discovered and my snooping confirmed, and Bridget doesn't strike me as the type of girl who bites when she kisses, which could work for or against me, I don't know.

I take my Curtis journal out of its hiding place and record the events of the day while Natalie munches cookies. I write: *Today I French kissed the rock star.* I always write "the rock star" instead of "Curtis," or "Curtis Piperfield," or "C.P." because I'm afraid that someday my house might burn down and the only thing I'd even attempt to save would be the Curtis journal, and if I passed out from smoke inhalation on the front lawn, clutching the journal, someone could easily get his hands on it and read it while I'm unconscious.

I write that Curtis tasted as if he'd just eaten something coconut, and that his hair smelled like baby shampoo. Also, that he doesn't feel as skinny as he looks.

This experience will probably be the subject of my next poem, and Sister Jude will probably have a coronary when she reads it. If I let her. I'm still not sure. Before I forget, I take the other poem out of my book bag and tape it to one of the journal pages.

Then I quote (or misquote) Curtis as saying "*Wow!*" instead of "*What the hell are you doing?*" When it comes to quoting the rock star, I tend to fudge a little. Okay, a lot. But it's not as if I've ever written: *The rock star had a difficult time unfastening my bra.* I just figure that if someone is going to go to all the trouble of keeping a secret journal that might one day be confiscated and read by the firelight of her burning home while she lies passed out in the grass, it might as well be interesting.

I am Curtis Piperfield's biggest fan, and fans tend to exaggerate. Can I help that?

~~~~~~~chapter 8

At 12:15 A.M., Cluck knocks on my window. He does this every time Natalie sleeps over. It's a tradition. I open the window and Cluck climbs in and shares popcorn or barbecue chips or cookies with us and we play Truth or Dare for about ninety seconds. It's no fun anymore because Cluck and Nat and I know everything about each other by now. Then Cluck leaves and Natalie and I change into our pajamas and go to bed.

My parents are oblivious to all of this. Their bedroom used to be across the hall, but a few years ago they added a master bedroom suite at the opposite end of the house. At first I was miffed that I had to stay in the same little room I'd always had, but the renovation wound up working to my advantage. I can talk on the phone, listen to the stereo, or sneak Cluck in at any hour of the day or night and my parents don't have a clue.

"Yow, C.C.," Cluck says, swinging his legs over the windowsill. "Got a surprise for you."

Patrick O'Connell sticks his face through my bedroom window. "Hi, C.C.," he says.

Before I scream at Cluck, I check three things:

Are my legs shaved? Yes. Good.

Is my underwear drawer closed? Yes. All the way? Yes. Good.

Have either Natalie or I farted in the room in the last three hours? No. Good.

When a boy (other than Cluck) slides into your bedroom at fifteen minutes past midnight, you want to be sure of these things. *Now* I scream at Cluck. "Are you crazy?"

He rolls his eyes. Cluck gets a real charge out of being in my bedroom. Apparently, so does Patrick, who looks dazed and really too happy for his own good. He is about to sit on my bed (sound familiar?), but I say, "Stop!" and point to the floor. Obediently, Patrick sits.

"Relax, C.C.," Cluck sort of coos in this breathy voice that he likes to use on me. If I were interested in Cluck I would probably find this sexy, but he's Cluck and I find it patronizing and annoying.

"You brought Patrick without my permission!" I say. But I'm not exactly mad. Finally, we can play Truth or Dare and get something out of it. Besides, Patrick looks good without his St. Simon Peter's blazer and tie. Really good.

I've been waiting for Cluck to arrive to tell him I French kissed the rock star, but with Patrick O'Connell practically drooling over me at the foot of my bed I decide not to mention it.

"Truth or Dare?" Nat suggests. So much for small talk.

Patrick's eyes light up. I mean *light up*!

"I'm first!" Nat squeals. "Cluck, truth or dare?"

"Truth."

"Bor-ing!"

"Okay, dare!"

"Good."

The dare is always the same. I don't mind. It's a good icebreaker, but it isn't as exciting as it was the first time. Nat smiles and Cluck knows what's coming and he doesn't mind either.

"Cluck, take off your shirt."

Patrick O'Connell eyes Cluck as if to say, "Hey, you weren't kidding," because he's obviously been alerted to the possibility of this happening. Patrick, I can tell, is hoping he'll get the same dare, and I decide that when it's my turn to do the daring, I'll happily oblige him. After all, he's been praying for me.

Cluck is a riot. He does a little striptease with his sweatshirt and everyone laughs. It's not a big deal because we see Cluck without a shirt practically all summer, but it's the way he de-shirts himself that makes it entertaining. And, to tell the truth, since Cluck's been playing lacrosse, he looks much more interesting with his shirt off. Of course, if he ever dares me or Nat to take our shirts off, we'll break his arm, lacrosse or not.

"My turn," I say. "Patrick, truth or dare?"

"Dare."

(What else?) It's not as easy to demand semi-nakedness of Patrick, and I stammer a little bit. "Take . . . um. Take off . . . I dare you to take off your shirt."

And—*whoosh*—it's off!

Patrick, who plays lacrosse and also swims for Simon Pete's, looks even better shirtless than Cluck does. He's wearing a gold chain with a crucifix on it, and Our Lord's feet are resting comfortably in the well-defined indentation between Patrick's pectoral muscles.

"Okay, C.C.," Cluck says, no longer cooing seductively at me. "Truth or dare?"

Something in his delivery makes me nervous. Usually I take dare, and when I do, Cluck challenges with a simple, "Kiss me," which is when the game ends and Cluck goes home. But tonight, I decide on truth.

"Cecily Carruthers, have you ever French kissed anyone?"

Patrick looks especially anxious to hear my response, but I notice he also looks as if he already knows the answer. I glance at Natalie. She looks as confused as me. She wouldn't have blabbed. Besides, she couldn't have blabbed. She's been with me from about three minutes after it happened. Then how do Cluck and Patrick know? Because, by now, I know they know.

"Yes," I admit. I want to sound as if it's no big deal, but I say this a little louder than I intended, which implies that it is a very big deal.

"Who?" they chorus. (But they must know this, too.)

"No fair, that's two questions. I answered Cluck's truth already."

Patrick looks right at me (he's got the greenest eyes I've ever seen) and goes, "Truth or dare, C.C."

I am now convinced that St. Simon Peter's Boys Prep offers an elective course called "Cooing," because Patrick says this to me in exactly the same smoky-sweet, just-barely-above-a-whisper voice that Cluck is so good at. I like how it sounds coming from Patrick, but I wish he hadn't used it for Truth or Dare.

"Dare," I say, and my voice sounds a little weird to me, as if it has melted.

Nothing is going through my mind. Nothing that should be, anyway, such as what if my mom or dad walks in and finds Nat and me with two half-naked Preppies? Instead, I'm wondering how many millions of sit-ups Patrick O'Connell has done in his lifetime to get his stomach to look like that.

"Okay," Patrick says. "I dare you to take a walk with me. Right now. Outside."

Cluck's eyes darken. He looks tense, and I figure he's thinking something along the lines of: Hold it one minute, Pat, old pal. This isn't the way we rehearsed it! You were supposed to find out about C.C.'s little game of tonsil hockey with Piperfield. We never agreed on you taking her for a walk. Alone. In the moonlight, for God's sake.

"Fine," I say. Patrick is on his feet and into his sweatshirt in seconds flat.

Sorry, Cluck, I'm thinking, but you should have

known better than to bring another guy into the bedroom of the girl you've loved since kindergarten, especially a guy who's been praying that nothing bad happens to the girl before he has a chance to—

But before I finish thinking, Patrick is helping me climb out of my bedroom window. Into the moonlight.

chapter 9 ━━━━━━━━

Patrick O'Connell was made for moonlight.

His hair is gleaming and his eyes seem to soak up the silver light from the moon.

We don't say a word until we're about fifty yards from the house. Then Patrick turns to me and says, "Curtis Piperfield says you Frenched him today."

It sounds so dumb. It sounds almost disgusting. I say, "I kissed him."

Patrick looks intrigued and crushed at the same time. "Curtis told Cluck. Cluck told me."

"Cluck told me you said a prayer for me in chapel." Even in the moonlight, I can tell he's blushing.

"I'm not in any hurry," he explains softly. "To . . . you know."

"Oh, I know. Me either."

"Me either."

"Good."

"Yeah." He steps closer to me. Just a little. "You really like Curtis Piperfield?"

I say this automatically: "I'm Curtis Piperfield's biggest fan. He's going to be a rock star."

"He likes Bridget Glenn."

"So I hear."

The air is damp and my legs are shaking, but I don't know if one has anything to do with the other.

Patrick slips back into that velvet voice and whispers, "Curtis told Cluck it was a terrific kiss."

I want to ask if Curtis mentioned any pain, say, from a small bite on the lip. But I don't. I can't.

Patrick takes my hand and he leans over and kisses me very softly. Then he does the weirdest thing: He just holds me.

Holds me. That sounds like something that happens between two people who are in love, but it's the only way I can describe it. He holds me and my face fits perfectly below his collarbone, where the crucifix (specifically Our Lord's right hand) is only sticking into my chin a little bit, but not enough to hurt.

Nine billion things occur to me at once: Patrick's lips are much softer than Curtis's; the *R* in his PREP SWIMMING sweatshirt is wearing off a little; Kelly Sinclair would probably kill for an opportunity like this; Curtis's first gold record will be dedicated to Bridget, not me; Sister Jude likes my poetry; I'm freezing (to name a few).

Then Patrick O'Connell from St. Simon Peter's Boys Prep lifts my chin and perfectly kisses me for almost eight-and-a-half minutes without stopping.

Before I allow myself to completely dissolve into Patrick's arms, I imagine Cluck watching us through the window and Natalie holding him by his high-tops to keep him from flying out into the moonlight to clobber Patrick.

I think I feel the world shifting to a slower spin. We are not just kissing, we are making out, and the moonlight drizzles down on us. I don't want the moment to end. I want Patrick to keep holding me and kissing me and touching my hair. And then it hits me.

Oh, God. I'm a nymphomaniac.

_____ chapter 10

Patrick helps me back in through the window, then climbs in behind me.

"Hey. We're back," he says.

Natalie is practically in a coma from all the junk food she's eaten while Pat and I were outside. Cluck is furious.

I say, "Whose turn is it?"

Cluck looks as if he's about to make a really snide comment, but all he says is, "C'mon, O'Connell. Let's go."

"Why?"

Cluck is halfway out the window. "Because." *Because you kissed Cecily Carruthers. Because you killed me.* I can almost hear him thinking it.

Patrick smiles at me. "See ya."

"Yeah."

When they're gone, Natalie says, "Wow!"

"What's that supposed to mean?" I ask. But I know. "Wow" is her commentary on the fact that her best friend has just French kissed two boys in one day—well, technically, since it's after midnight, two days.

Natalie shrugs. "I'm going to the Bernie Formal."

I look at her hard. "With *who*?"

"Frankie Bruno. Cluck says he's going to ask me."

Just like that. No kissing. No climbing out windows. All I can think of to say is, "Wow."

"Yeah, well." We're quiet for a few seconds. Natalie changes into her pajamas and slithers into her sleeping bag. "'Night, C.C."

"'Night." I don't bother to change. I crawl into bed with my clothes on, still shivery from the damp air, Pat's kissing, and Cluck's "Because." *Because.* It sounded so final. "Nat?"

"Mmmm?"

"Do you think Cluck will come over next Saturday night?"

"Maybe. Maybe not."

Thanks a lot, Natalie. Have a diet root beer, why don't you? "But do you *think* he will?"

She's probably hoping that he will, and that this time he'll bring good old Frankie Bruno through my bedroom window with him. In a minute she says, "He could always go to Kelly Sinclair's. After all."

That night, I dream that every student at St. Simon Peter's climbs through my bedroom window. They're like Preppie warriors, whirling their neckties in the air. They are bare-chested and awful. Some awfully good, some awfully bad, but the sight of them is terrifying. Sal Malanconico is there, carrying a dictionary in which all the dirty words have been underlined. And Cluck is there, too. He is whispering "Yow," in a very sexy voice. Then Sister Jude appears and begins reading poetry to them, which causes them to evaporate slowly, until the only thing left is a smoldering pile of puke-plaid ties on my bedroom floor. I wake up sweating, and the pile turns out to be my best friend, sitting up in her sleeping bag.

"Mother of God! It's four in the morning. What were you screaming about?"

"Nightmare," I tell her.

Natalie rolls over in her bag. "They say too much kissing'll do that to you."

"Funny." I lie back down in bed. "Do you even *like* Frankie Bruno?" I ask her. She fiddles with the zipper on her sleeping bag. I take this as a yes.

The moon is low in the sky, dead center in my window, and almost full. It is the same moon that is shining on Cluck's house around the corner, on Curtis Piperfield's house across the street, and on Bridget's breasts a few blocks away (that is, if she happens to be awake at this hour and standing outside in the nude). But most of all, the moon in my window is the same moon that glowed in Patrick O'Connell's eyes. I have a sudden, sweet feeling of togetherness, which soothes me back to sleep.

■

On Sunday morning, I go to 8:00 mass with my parents as usual, and we leave Natalie sleeping in a lump on my bedroom floor.

Mr. McNally and Cluck's little brother Sean are in the pew ahead of us. Cluck always sleeps in on Sundays and comes to 10:15 mass with his mother and four sisters. Catholics are very predictable, thank God. I could not face offering Cluck the sign of peace this morning—although I get the feeling our relationship could use it. It is difficult enough shaking hands with Sean.

Patrick O'Connell's mother is a eucharistic minister and serves 12:00 mass, so that's when *they* go.

Curtis is a Methodist.

I wake up Nat when we get home. While she's showering, I make an entry in my Curtis journal: *The moon on his roof is musical.*

But last night, the moon was more for Patrick than for Curtis. For some reason, this gives me a strange, lonely feeling, the kind of feeling you get when you finish reading a book you really like, the feeling that something's ending, changing, and you can't do anything about it. Maybe it's just guilt over writing Patrick thoughts in Curtis's book, but I remember the moon and I can't help it. I also can't help the incredible growling in my stomach, and I wish Nat would hurry up so we could have breakfast. I'm starving.

In the interest of loyalty, I close my Curtis journal and pick up my English notebook, because I suspect there's a poem about to happen and the possibility exists that it might be about Patrick. But as it turns out, it's about me. Me and the moon.

I have bitten the moon
Now it rots to its rind in the sky,
Bleeds silver nectar to clot among the clouds.
There is moonflesh on my lips;
Night trickles down my chin.
I only wanted a taste.

I read the poem out loud and decide Sister Jude will love "moonflesh." That is, if I decide to show her the poem.

Finally, Natalie appears in her bathrobe and says, "Let's eat."

Usually we have French toast because we learned how to make it in Girl Scouts in fourth grade. But today, I am boycotting anything French: toast, poodles, fries, kisses . . .

"How about omelettes, Nat?"

"Sure."

I begin scrambling eggs and repeat the question she never answered the night before. "So, do you even *like* Frankie Bruno?"

Nat says she wants to walk by the junior high later, to see if Frankie is shooting baskets with Walter Mert. This is definitely a yes.

I keep scrambling. Since Natalie was never overly

supportive of me regarding Curtis, I'm a little put out that she expects me to be a party to this. But she is my best friend, so after breakfast, we go.

On the way, I mention that I've always been of the opinion that Frankie Bruno has big nostrils. I don't mean this in a cruel way, of course.

Nat keeps walking. "Never noticed." (I must admit, Natalie is much better than I am at accepting criticism.)

Frankie is dribbling with Walter Mert. He has his Simon Pete's baseball jacket tied around his waist. Nice nostrils, I am thinking. But he's really not a bad guy.

He waves. Nat waves. Walter waves. I don't bother.

Frankie misses the ball on purpose so it bounces in our direction. This is my cue. I say I am going to get a drink from the water fountain. Naturally, this is a big fib. I would never put my lips on the spout of a drinking fountain. God only knows how many different people have been slurping on it. I suppose, today, the same could be said of my lips.

When I return, Natalie says, "Guess what."

I can't imagine. "Congratulations," I say. "I hope you have a great time."

We start walking and I notice that Natalie, who

is normally the most straightforward human being alive, is shuffling her feet. I know she's holding something back.

"What else?"

She looks up. "We're going to double. With Cluck. And Kelly."

This is like a knife in the back. Not an especially sharp knife. After all, it wasn't her idea, and it's not as if I wanted to go with Cluck. But it does hurt a little, being left out. I say, "That's nice." And I try not to sound upset.

"Maybe we can triple. You can come with us. You and . . ."

". . . And?"

"Oh. I see what you mean."

I wonder. Does she?

━━━━━━━━chapter 11

"Bless me, Father, for I have . . ."

. . . Frenched?

No.

It is Sunday night and I am lying in bed, practicing for tomorrow morning when I will slip into chapel for a nice, early, soul-cleansing confession with good old Father Wink. My window is open, and across the street I can hear Curtis playing his guitar. Normally this gives me great chills, but it's hard to be a rock star fanatic when you're practicing for confession.

Good old Father Wink is actually Father Mario Bertolli, our chaplain. The students at St. B.'s nicknamed him Wink because he has this nervous tic that makes his eye blink. He also whistles through his teeth when he pronounces his *s*'s, so whenever he says "Our Lord, Jesus Christ," it sounds as though he's deflating through a slow leak.

Father Wink is about nine thousand years old, and I think most of the nuns at St. Bernadette's could beat him up. But everyone likes him. He doesn't mind being called Wink, either. He coaches varsity field hockey, and for an old guy he's got a lot of spirit. He has these two lucky hats he wears to all the games—one for home games, one for away. Once I told my dad I thought Father Wink would make a good pope, mostly because he's such a sweet old duffer, but also because he looks especially good in hats. I believe that anybody even thinking about becoming pope should really be a hat person.

I fluff up my pillow and give it another try.

"Bless me, Father, for I'm a nymphomaniac."

Absolutely not. I yawn and roll over, searching for the appropriate words. Where's old Sal Malanconico when you need him, anyway? I fall asleep wondering what Father Wink will think of me when he learns that I French kissed two boys in one day.

■

Every girl at St. Bernadette's dreams of getting married in our school chapel—most of them to Cluck. The chapel is small and smells like just-blown-out candles, and the sun pours in through the stained-glass windows and makes puddles of color on the pews, the altar, and the big crucifix behind it. Once, during morning prayer, when the sun was at just the precise angle to splash Christ with splotches of red, gold, green, and blue, I whispered to Grace Boccaluzzo that it looked as if Our Lord was wearing a tie-dyed t-shirt.

"Last summer I saw Gilbert wearing a tie-dyed t-shirt," Grace whispered back, which shows you where her mind was.

Today, it is pouring outside, and the only color washing into the chapel is gray.

The light over Father Wink's confessional is on, and I brush the curtain aside and go in. "Bless me, Father, for I have sinned. It's been . . . um, a month since my last . . . since my . . ."

"Relax, child," Father says. He calls everyone child. It's old-fashioned, but it makes you feel kind of good. He is speaking in the special tone of voice that is reserved for talking to sinners. It is probably a required class at the seminary.

Even through the little screen, I am pretty sure

he knows it's me. But I tell him anyway. "Father . . . it's me. Cecily Carruthers."

"Good morning, Cecily."

"I hope that isn't illegal, telling you my name."

"No it's perfectly all right. Would you feel more comfortable, perhaps, if we sat in my office and did this face-to-face?" His *s*'s come whistling out at me. I feel as if I am confessing to a parakeet.

"Thanks, but I'm sort of a traditionalist. I just wanted you to know it was me." For a moment, I think I might just forget the whole thing and tell him I only stopped by to say how much I admire the field hockey team's new uniforms. But there's no use prolonging the agony. I take a deep breath.

"Father, I did this really awful thing. I don't know if it's a sin. Maybe it's just a little one; you know, a menial sin."

"Venial, child."

"Yeah. Venial. Well, it all started three years ago when Curtis Piperfield told me he was going to be a rock star and I decided to be his biggest fan. And then, just this past Saturday, I snuck into his room and got in his bed—*he* wasn't in his bed, though, Father, he wasn't even *home*—but then he came in and caught me reading this stupid note from Bridget Glenn and he was pretty mad. And then I kissed him."

Father says, "I see."

"*French* kissed him, Father." I was pretty sure it made a difference.

"I see."

"Then that night, I did it again. I French kissed again, but not with Curtis, with Patrick O'Connell. Outside. In the moonlight." Then I add, in case it will help, "Patrick is Catholic." *Then* I add, "Oh, and I lied to Mrs. Piperfield. About a Tupperware bowl. With a lid."

"Hmmmm," comes Father Wink's voice through the screen.

I am wondering when I started to cry. Probably just before "moonlight."

"Father Wink . . . am I going to Hell?"

Then something happens that, to the best of my knowledge, has never before happened in the confessional. Father Wink starts to laugh. Not *at* me, like "Ha ha, you're gonna get it." Just a small, gentle laugh.

"Am I?"

"Dear, dear Cecily Carruthers." He clasps his hands together. "Hell would not take you."

I'm not exactly sure what he means by this. "But I . . ."

"It's all right, child. Kissing is not so awful. I promise."

"Then how come I feel so crummy?"

"You're confused, Cecily. Confusion is not a sin. I'm sure your intentions were pure."

Personally, I have my doubts about that, but I don't say so. "Can I do it again?" This question is out before I can stop myself. Well, I suppose it couldn't hurt to ask.

Through the screen I see his outline. He is touching the tips of his fingers together. "Oh, I'm pretty certain that you will." He pauses, shifting in his seat. "The Lord Our God has given us a great responsibility. He's given us judgment and free will." He's also given us Patrick O'Connell's pectoral muscles, I am thinking. "It's easy to become confused. Especially when we are young. But we must remember His words: 'Lead us not into temptation.'"

"Yes, Father."

"Control, Cecily. You must learn to control yourself."

"I will."

Good old Father Wink gives me three Hail Marys

and an Apostle's Creed—for lying. I guess he considers the kissing a first (and second) offense.

I am absolved of my sins. So I go to algebra.

chapter 12 〰〰〰〰〰〰

By lunch, it's all over school that I kissed Patrick. Frankie Bruno's sister Lisa, who is a junior at St. Bernie's, found out somehow and told everybody. I don't know who told Lisa. I hope it wasn't Patrick. But believe me, this kind of stuff gets around. The only good thing about it is that Lisa and all her friends are extremely jealous.

Grace Boccaluzzo is a little miffed that I didn't call her to tell her about it the second Patrick took his tongue out of my mouth.

"It was almost one o'clock in the morning, Grace."

"You could have called the next day."

"Sorry."

Grace is sulking over her pickle and pimento-loaf sandwich. She is not just mad that I didn't tell her that Pat kissed me, she is mad *because* Pat kissed me. After Cluck, Patrick O'Connell is the St. Simon Peter's guy the Bernie Girls think about most. Grace is cute, but not Pat's type, which happens to be the same as Cluck's type: me. This is not conceit, this is fact.

"Here," I say. "Have a Frito." I hope this will pass for an olive branch.

"Thanks." Grace warms up. She wants details. "How long? How wet?"

I smile, just thinking about it. "Pretty long," I tell her. "And just wet enough."

Grace says she would like to be kissed by Gilbert like that. Suddenly I realize it's 12:08 and I haven't called him yet.

"Hi, C.C." No *yow.* No *how's my girl.* After what happened Saturday night with Patrick, I guess Cluck is finally convinced that I am not his girl.

"Hi, Cluck."

"Is Kelly around?"

Ouch. It's not like Cluck to be spiteful. Kelly is less than two feet away from me at the juice machine but I say, "Nope, don't see her." Now it's my turn. "Is Patrick around?" I know it's cruel, but that's what he gets for being such a jerk.

On the other end of the phone, I can tell that Cluck has started a slow burn. "Damn it, C.C." Then before I can tell him to quit cussing, he says, "Truth or dare?"

Talk about your no-win situations. I swallow hard and mumble, "Truth."

"What about me?" Cluck says. But he doesn't wait for an answer, I guess because I've already given him one. He hangs up without saying good-bye.

■

Lisa Bruno takes me aside in the locker room after gym and wants to know if Patrick and I are an item.

"A what?"

Lisa rolls her eyes, but I know what she means: An *item* is the junior class's current euphemism for two kids who've been kissing. "Has he called you? Is he taking you to the formal?"

Is it any of her business? Father Wink didn't ask this many questions. I pretend not to hear her over the banging of lockers and leave as fast as I can.

I am not in the mood for religion. The class, I

mean. With my luck, Sister Marie Ignatius will be giving a lecture on Mary Magdalene and I'll spend the rest of the day ducking imaginary stones. I tell Sister I've got a stomachache, which isn't exactly a lie, and spend the period in the nurse's office.

After the nurse takes my temperature (the school nurse would take your temperature if you had a fractured skull), she puts me in a room with a cot and closes the door. I flip open my English notebook and start work on a new poem. The poem is confused, I guess because I'm confused. It is mostly about Patrick, but there are some references to Curtis in there as well, which is a pretty accurate reflection of the way I've been feeling. Boy, you can't hide anything from a poem, same as you can't hide anything from Sister Jude.

THIS,

This is love.
It is that boy with the mangled romance
He receives the gift

She has tied up her innocence
In a shy parcel

The boy wears clever blue jeans
And the rock 'n' roll wilts

It is that boy with the dusty voice
His lips are as soft as moonlight
The darkness comes out of his eyes
            and covers her
She hardly remembers
If he is blond.

I hide out in the nurse's office until halfway through the last period of the day. Sister Jude isn't in her classroom, but I find her in the teacher's lounge, sitting quietly on a sofa.

"Sister Jude?"

"Come in, C.C."

I am holding the poem behind my back. "I wrote another poem."

"I thought you would."

"Right. Well. Would you like to read it?"

She stands, smiling. "Of course." She takes it. Carefully. In a way that implies great respect, as if it would turn to ash and blow away if she accidentally dropped it.

Me, I've been folding it and unfolding it and sweating on it with my clammy hands.

She leans against the windowsill, and sun spills in on the paper as if maybe God is reading over her shoulder. That's a pretty dramatic statement, I admit, but that's what it looks like. Sister notices, too. "'A certain slant of light . . .'" she says.

"Pardon?"

"That's a line from a poem. By Emily Dickinson."

"Oh. Yeah." The reference is lost on me, but I try not to let on. She goes back to the poem with the sun on it. "It's not that good," I say for the heck of it.

"Nonsense."

Does she mean, nonsense, it *is* that good, or nonsense, the *poem* is nonsense? I can't tell. I want it to be good. Maybe I need it to be good. I know I need something, something to make me a little bit special other than the fact that I do not dot my *i*'s with little hearts and that I may be slightly liberal when it comes to kissing boys.

Sister Jude looks up from the paper. "You are an imagist, C.C."

I am a ninth grader. I am Curtis Piperfield's biggest fan. I am also a nymphet-in-training, I suppose. Now I'm an imagist? "What's that?"

"The way you are able to use words to make pictures, to create images. 'Clever blue jeans' is a wonderful line. It reminds me of my favorite pair."

This takes me by surprise and I blurt out, "You have blue jeans?"

She nods. "I wear them for gardening at my parents' house."

I almost blurt out, "You have *parents?!*" but I control myself. Father Wink would be proud. "I'm glad you like it."

I stand there for a minute or two, and I know she's looking through my head again. Finally, she says, "Is anything wrong?"

This comes out in a whisper: "Everything."

"Would you like to talk about it?"

"Not yet."

She nods. "When you're ready."

"Thank you." She hands me the poem. "And thanks for reading this." I walk toward the door, but before I step out into the hallway, I turn and ask, "May I read some of your poetry sometime?" I don't know how I know she writes poetry, I just know.

"By all means."

I bet somewhere out there is a man who was probably nuts in love with Sister Jude Thaddeus when she was a regular girl with a regular girl's name, wearing blue jeans and writing poetry. And

I bet he still wonders about her and wishes things were different.

You never think about nuns having lives before the convent, but they must, right? They must.

I escape St. Bernadette's through the side door about fifteen.

chapter 13 ~~~~~~~~~~

I escape St. Bernadette's through the side door about fifteen minutes before dismissal.

When I left Sister Jude in the teacher's lounge, I'd fully intended to make an appearance in my last period class, but there is no hall monitor in sight and I take this as a kind of sign. I push open the door; the rain has stopped and the day welcomes me. Warm, windy, full of promise, and suddenly full of Patrick, who is leaning against the statue of St. Bernadette.

He waves.

I wave and hope I don't drop dead from shock. "Hi."

"Hi." Pat is careful not to tromp on the geraniums that have been newly planted in three wide crescents at the saint's feet. Cluck would have jumped over them, just to show that he could. Salvatore Malanconico would have trampled them, on purpose. Pat is too sweet to do either of those things. He negotiates St. Bernadette's modest, muddy garden respectfully. His hands are in his pockets, his tie loosened around his neck.

"I was waiting for you," he says. "I didn't expect you to be out so early."

I almost wish I'd stayed inside until the bell, so all those creepy juniors and Kelly Sinclair could have seen Patrick O'Connell leaning against our patron saint, waiting to meet me.

"Are you ditching last period?" I ask, but I know that any guy considerate enough to tiptoe through a bed of scrawny geraniums doesn't have a ditching bone in his body.

"No. I have study hall. I got a pass."

"How come?" I ask, just to hear him say it.

"So I could walk you home."

Perfect. Perfect words, perfect delivery, perfect day. I send up a quick prayer that my skirt doesn't blow up in the breeze. The sun is warm on my face; I am tingling. I start off down the sidewalk, and he falls into step alongside me.

"I just want you to know that I didn't tell anyone about Saturday," he says gently.

I bite my lip. "Somebody told somebody. And that somebody told everybody."

"Yeah, I know. I'm really sorry. But it wasn't me."

"I didn't think it was." Suddenly, I stop short.

"What?"

My eyes are wide. "Cluck told."

Pat looks down at his shoes and says nothing.

"Didn't he?"

Pat shrugs. "Don't be mad at him."

I feel as if I've been socked in the stomach. Cluck McNally, the boy who has supposedly dedicated his heart and soul to me, the boy who asked me to marry him three hundred and twenty-seven times, the boy I've known since kindergarten—*Cluck*—told. Tears sting behind my eyes. "Aren't you?" I demand. "Aren't you mad at him?" I am suddenly desperate for loyalty.

"Well, yeah, of course I'm mad at him."

"Okay, then why can't I be mad at him? It's only fair." I start walking again, and Patrick reaches out and puts his hands on my shoulders.

"Wait, C.C. Think about it. Cluck is crazy about you."

"I'm aware of that, Patrick, thank you."

Pat releases me and I walk away. After about

five steps I notice he is not with me. Wonderful. Doesn't he know he's supposed to be following me? Now what do I do? I can't stop, because that would mess up my dramatic exit; it would kill the rhythm. It's his turn, he should call out my name, tell me to stop, take me in his arms, kiss me. He's not supposed to just *stand* there. I slow down a little, hoping he figures it out.

"C.C."

Finally. I stop, but don't face him. "What?"

"Don't leave, okay? Please?" His voice is soft, creamy.

"Okay."

I wouldn't leave Patrick O'Connell for ten million bucks. But of course he doesn't know that. We walk to my house quietly, our fingertips almost touching, and I ask him in, even though my mom isn't home and this could get me grounded for the rest of my life.

The second Pat steps through the door, I panic. Except for Cluck, I've never had a boy over before. Should I do something? Make something? The only thing I'm good at is French toast, and that would be stupid.

We go into the family room, where the components of my mom's religion-specific bulletin board are still cluttering the coffee table. Patrick sits on the couch and examines a pile of construction-paper letters.

"They're going to spell Hallelujah," I explain. "Want a soda?"

"Sure."

I go to the kitchen. There's only one Coke in the refrigerator. One Coke and a diet root beer that Natalie left. I would let myself dehydrate before I would drink a diet root beer in front of Patrick O'Connell. I plunk some ice cubes in a glass, and while I pour the soda, my mind races.

Should I change my clothes? Natalie would know, wardrobe is her department. But she's not home, she's got piano today.

And now that Patrick is here, what are we supposed to *do*? Make out? Does he expect to sit around and kiss? Does he think just because it happened that one time, it's going to happen again? Not that it wouldn't be great!

Control, C.C.

Just in case, though, I cup my hands together and blow into them to check my breath. But this never works, so I hope for the best and go back to the family room.

I hand him the Coke and sit down beside him. This is *so* weird. "How's lacrosse?" I ask him.

"It's great. I'm the only freshman that gets to play varsity." He blushes.

"Wow." Curtis never blushed in front of me.

"Maybe you can come and see us play sometime."

Cluck has been nagging me to come to a lacrosse game forever, and until now, I've had no trouble resisting. "Sure," I tell Patrick. "Anytime."

"Great." He takes a long drink. "I really can't stay, C.C. I'm meeting Walter at the junior high to shoot baskets."

That Walter, he gets along with everybody.

"Oh," I say. "Okay."

But Patrick does not get up to leave. He stays on the couch. Then he leans forward and picks up the pile of letters for the bulletin board. "You're missing an *L*," he says.

"Excuse me?"

He fans out the letters like a poker hand. "Hallelujah. It has three *L*'s. There're only two here."

"Oh, right. Thanks."

"Yeah, well, I'm a pretty good speller." He feels ridiculous, I can tell. "I'm kind of a word person."

"Me, too." I'm about to ask his position on poetry, but I don't get the chance.

"I was wondering if you'd like to go to the spring formal with me," he says.

Talk about poetry! Those are the most beautiful words I've ever heard.

"That'd be great."

"Yeah, great." Patrick is smiling. His eyes are fabulous and they remind me of the moonlight. He pushes my hair back a little. Then he kisses my forehead, which sends this shiver through my entire body.

I walk him to the door in a daze. Some female instinct tells me to say, "Call me."

And Patrick says, "Definitely." Then he stands on the front steps for a second, smiling at me with the sun in his hair. I imagine Walter is getting a little ticked by now. Who cares?

"Bye, C.C.," Pat says, backing down the steps with his hands in his pockets. He continues backward down the walk, as if it would be painful to take his eyes off of me.

"Bye."

Patrick O'Connell is taking me to the spring formal. Hallelujah.

————————chapter 14

As soon as Patrick is out of sight, I make a mad dash to the bus stop to wait for Natalie. I am betting that today she will have on one of her sexier ensembles because she knows that Frankie Bruno will be at the burger place.

I know, of course, that Curtis Piperfield will be getting off the Miltondale bus, too, and that he will have on very clever blue jeans, and look as rock-starish as an eighth grader possibly can. He may also have a note from Bridget Glenn in his clever pocket, who knows?

I'm scared, but I want to get it over with.

Cluck shows up and says, "Waiting for Nat?"

I nod. "And the rock star."

Cluck sits beside me on the curb. "Forget Curtis. And forget Patrick, damn it."

"Don't cuss," I tell him, then I raise one eyebrow and ask, "Is Patrick going to forget me?" I say this in a very snippy tone. I happen to know that Patrick is not going to forget me, not even if he lives to be a hundred and one.

Cluck shakes his head. "Doubt it."

"Are you planning to forget Kelly Sinclair?" Also snippy.

"Eventually."

Cluck doesn't ask me to go for sodas. Not that I would go anyway, because I am furious with him. "You told."

"Yeah, I told." He sounds sorry. He is sitting with his knees pulled up and his arms around them. He is staring into the street.

"That was crummy, Cluck."

"Yes, it was." There is a cold, enormous silence between us. "Do you hate me?" he wants to know and drags his hand through his hair.

"I wouldn't know how to hate you," I admit.

"Good." Cluck's hair is longer than it's ever been, but he does not appear to be enjoying any sort of power at this moment. He looks sad and alone. Sad and alone and afraid. "I watched you kiss him, you know."

I figured as much. "That's sort of obscene, Cluck."

"I didn't mean to watch. I just looked out the window and there you were. Kissing."

I repeat what I learned from Father Wink in confession. "Kissing is not so awful."

He gives me a sideways look and a grin and says, "It sure as hell didn't look awful."

The old Cluck returns. "Don't cuss," I tell him. "And don't be sick." Then something occurs to me. "Do *you* hate *me*?"

Cluck doesn't answer right away, but I'm pretty sure he couldn't hate me any more than I could hate him.

At that moment, the Miltondale Junior High School bus putters to a halt and the doors shriek open and Natalie appears, looking weird. Happy. Surprised. Mostly weird. She gives me a secret best-friend message with her eyes, which I decipher as *Curtis Piperfield is going to ask you to go for sodas.*

Then Curtis emerges and for the first time ever, he stops at the curb.

"Hi, C.C.," he says. "Wanna go get a soda?"

I probably should say, "What the hell are you doing?" instead of answering his question, because that's how he answered *my* question about the dance the day I kissed him. But I am still a loyal fan—or a curious one, at least—and I say, "Sure."

Clearly, this is just too much for Cluck to take. He stands up and looks me straight in the eye. "Yeah, C.C." he says. "Yeah, I do hate you." Then he takes off down the street at top speed.

Am I having an unbelievable day, or what?

Natalie watches Cluck sprint away. Then she turns back to me. I sigh, sending my bangs into a flutter. I had wanted to tell her about Patrick asking me to the formal, but Curtis is waiting. I tell her I'll call her. As always, Nat understands.

Curtis and I walk to the burger place. On the way, he says, "Thank you for kissing me. I liked it."

"I didn't bite you, did I?"

Curtis shakes his head. "You must really like me."

It's not a question. It's a statement of fact. I don't respond. I am noticing that Curtis doesn't have half the caliber of upper body that Patrick O'Connell has. But then, Curtis is probably thinking the exact same thing about me in comparison to Bridget Glenn.

"I know you like Bridget," I say. Now he nods.

We don't say anything for the rest of the walk, and I'm remembering something I heard once about wishes: Be careful what you wish for, you just might get it. I used to think that was the stupidest saying, but today it makes sense. Last Friday I would have begged, borrowed, stolen—or kissed—to get Curtis to take me for sodas. Today, I am thinking I could be walking by the junior high right now, watching Patrick shoot baskets with Walter.

We finally get to the burger place. More boys than usual say hello to me when I walk in, and this makes my skin crawl. I follow Curtis to a booth and sit down. When the sodas come, Curtis says, "I'm not going to be a rock star, C.C."

At this I just about bite through my straw, doing some minimal damage to my tongue, which—judging from the way the Preppies are staring—has become a legend at Simon Pete's. "You're not?" I choke out.

Curtis shakes his head. "I'm going to be a certified public accountant."

I take a huge swallow of soda to wash down the news. This is the most unbelievable thing I've ever heard. But what's more, it has caused me to feel the most unbelievable thing I've ever felt:

Nothing.

It's as if all my emotions are sitting around looking at each other saying, "So what?" That's how I feel—very *so what?*

So I say, "So what?"

"So I thought it would make a difference."

Wrong, Curtis, I am thinking. The difference

was made shortly after midnight on Saturday when Patrick O'Connell put his arms around me. I realize now that I even could have done without Pat's kissing, nice as it was, and been deliriously content with him just holding me. A person holding you can make a lot of difference.

And suddenly, I agree with Natalie. Curtis is a little young and way too skinny.

"What changed your mind?" I ask, merely out of curiosity.

Curtis shrugs. "Bridget, I guess. She hates loud music. She's not too crazy about rock 'n' roll."

I withdraw my opinion that Curtis is an artist. An artist would never surrender his art for a seventh grader with breasts, I'm sure of it. Too bad, too, because Curtis had real talent. He was great on the guitar.

The bill for the sodas arrives. Apparently, we're splitting it because Curtis asks, "What's two fifty-eight divided by two?"

I have some serious reservations regarding Curtis's success as an accountant. I hand him a dollar twenty-nine, and when we stand up to leave, Curtis says, "It was a terrific kiss."

I smile at him but my emotions are still going *so what?*

~~~~~~~~~~~~chapter 15

"Go away, C.C.," Cluck says when I show up at his house. "Go find Curtis."

"Forget Curtis," I tell him. "I just found something out and I want to teach it to you."

"Go find Patrick."

He is leaning in his doorway. I am on the front porch. "Cluck, listen to me. It's important." All of a sudden I think of something. "Why do we call you Cluck?"

"Because."

"Because why?"

"Would you want to be called Gilbert?"

"That's not the reason."

He steps onto the porch. "Damn it, C.C."

"Don't *cuss*!"

"Do you really want to know?" I nod. "Okay. When we were in second grade, remember our communion class? Frankie Bruno dared me to corner you behind the baptismal font and kiss you."

"And?"

"I didn't." Of course he didn't; I would have remembered that. "So Frankie and those guys started calling me chicken."

"Oh."

"And then they started making chicken sounds, you know, clucking at me. And after that, they just called me . . ."

". . . Cluck."

"Cluck. You named me, C.C. Indirectly."

"Wow. Sorry."

Cluck sits down on the step. "I didn't mind, since it was in your honor. Sort of."

Then I remember the note I sent to Curtis. I wanted to name his band, but I didn't exactly know why until now: When you name something, it's yours forever. Names are permanent and intimate. Maybe that's why it spooks me that sister Jude calls me C.C.—it shows she knows who I really am. No wonder Cluck loves me; I named him.

"Gilbert, this is what I've learned. You don't love

me. You love the idea of me. The way I loved the idea of the rock star."

He shakes his head. "No, C.C. I think I really love you."

I sit down next to him. "How do you know?"

He thinks before he answers. "Because every time I see you, I feel like I'm just learning to breathe."

"Oh."

"And because the night you kissed Patrick, I forgot."

"Forgot what?"

"How to breathe."

We share another silence, but this one is not ugly, like the one at the bus stop. Then Cluck does the weirdest thing. If anyone had said to me, you can have five thousand dollars if you can guess what Cluck is going to do next, I wouldn't have been able to do it. He stretches out on the porch step and puts his head in my lap.

His head. *In my lap.*

But the funny thing is, it doesn't feel disgusting or even sexy. It feels like Cluck, with his head in my lap. Automatically, I push the hair off his forehead and he closes his eyes.

"I need a haircut."

"Maybe just a trim."

"Remember the time we smoked cigarettes?" He is smiling. I nod, but his eyes are still closed. "It was your idea, remember?"

We were eleven. That was my dangerous summer. I dared Cluck to shoplift a Milky Way from Durgan's, and he did. We didn't get caught, but we got our butts to confession fast and never did it again. Then one Sunday, we smoked cigarettes in an empty lot near the beach where the high school kids went parking. We weren't supposed to ride our bikes any farther than the burger place, but I talked Cluck into riding all the way to the shore. Cluck gave me a ring that day. It was fake, naturally, because we were eleven, but I knew that to him it was worth about a trillion bucks.

"Everything I ever did, I did with you," he says, and it sounds like a poem.

He is still lying there, with his head in my lap. I am about to tell him to sit up, but I decide to just shut up. I have never seen Cluck look so comfortable. So comforted.

"What do you love about Patrick?" he asks me.

"Everything. What do you love about Kelly Sinclair?"

"Nothing. But I would still like to kiss her."

"It takes time, Cluck."

"What does? Kissing?"

"Kissing takes time. Forgetting takes time." And I should know. It's taken me this long to forget Curtis Piperfield. And I know that it will probably take a while for Cluck to forget me, a thought that comes like a note of sad piano music. I pause; my fingers are still now, lingering in his hair. "Remembering takes time, too," I tell him. And I know *this* because right now I am remembering.

TOBACCO
For Cluck

The day we were wild
We smoked Camels
In a cleft of lilac,
Two dappled pretty knees
Two scraped ones, yours,
In the green shade and pinkening smoke
The leaves swelled white underbellies
Like lace

In your heart
I married you,

95

That dangerous morning,
All young and Sunday.
I wore your ring—
A slip of gold
One ruby set with pearls—
We snuffed secrets
In the loose dirt

And the sky ladled heat.

We hid
Where the mountain laurel
Wound up and around
The salt-stung blond lots
And skimmed our childhoods away
Like stones across a quiet tide
Until the cool came glittering.

In a breath
We found autumn.

chapter 16

Natalie could wear a different outfit every day for twelve years, maybe thirteen, that's how many clothes she has. It is one week before the formal, and we are searching her vast wardrobe for something I can wear. Right now I've got on this flowery number that makes me look like Chiquita Banana's sidekick. I shake my head. "Don't think so. Next?"

Natalie hands me a little, black, strapless deal which she describes as simple and elegant. The designer had Bridget Glenn in mind when he made it, I guess, because the cups are *hu-mun-go* sized.

"I wish. Next?"

The next dress is plaid. Not puke-plaid, but plaid. Close enough. "*Next!*"

Natalie rummages through the closet, and I stare at myself in the full-length mirror on the back of the door. My St. Bernie's uniform is in a pile at my feet, as if I care what happens to it, right? I want Natalie's wardrobe. I *covet* Natalie's wardrobe. That's probably good for five Hail Marys at least.

I try on the next dress. Natalie says it's a classic, you can tell by the cuffs. The dress after that is ultra-feminine (Natalie's word, not mine). The dress after that is trendy. I am getting frustrated. The classic dress was boring; the ultra-feminine dress reminded me of Kelly Sinclair; and as far as the trendy one is concerned, my father would never let me out of the house in it.

Natalie dives back into her closet. Never say die, that's Natalie's motto when it comes to wardrobe. Her voice is muffled; I think she is extolling the virtues of linen.

I unzip the trendy number and say, "In the old days, when my mom was in Catholic school, they had to kneel down in homeroom every day. Guess why?"

Natalie emerges with a flowing, silky thing in a soft blue. "To pray."

"Nope. To have their skirts measured. If the

hem didn't touch the floor, they got sent home to change."

Natalie rolls her eyes. "Mother of God."

I try on the blue dress and decide it's not me, but for some reason I picture it being the sort of dress Sister Jude might wear if she weren't a nun.

Natalie makes a face. "Take it off. You look like the tooth fairy on a bad day."

I wonder if she goes through this every morning, getting dressed for Miltondale, and I think, puke-plaid or not, my St. Bernie's uniform is good for something.

•

The next day, I finish my homework in study hall and ask Sister Marie Ignatius for a pass to see Sister Jude. Sister Marie Iggy assumes that I am going for extra help, which I sort of am; I want Sister Jude's opinion on the poem I wrote for Cluck. Sister Marie writes the pass and hands it to me as if she's doing me this huge favor for which I should be eternally grateful.

Sister Jude is correcting sophomore essays when I arrive in the doorway. She asks me if I'd like to take a walk around the grounds; it's too beautiful to stay indoors.

I'm sure the other girls will think I'm trying to score brownie points if they see me walking around with her, or they may even wonder if I'm considering becoming a nun. Fat chance. I've grown pretty fond of kissing, if you want to know the truth.

Sister Jude has brought along a package of strawberry licorice. "Would you like one?" She hands me a licorice stick.

"Thanks." We pass the marble statue of St. Bernadette at the main entrance of the school.

"Is everything still wrong?" she asks out of nowhere.

"Huh? Oh, you mean . . . no, actually things are better. Thanks for asking."

"Did you get any good poems out of it?"

"Out of what?"

"Out of things being wrong. That's usually good inspiration."

"Well, it was mostly boy problems," I confess.

"Oh, well then, you must have written something wonderful! Boy problems are the best inspiration there is."

This stuns me. I don't know any tactful way to

ask her how she would know, so I simply say, "How do you know?" and hope it's not too disrespectful. I am dying to hear the answer.

Sister Jude examines her fingernails. "I had a pretty serious boyfriend in college. I wasn't always a nun, you know. In fact, I wanted to be an actress."

"Get *out*!" Immediately, my hand flies to my mouth. I just said "Get out" to a nun.

"I was a theater major," she says. "That was before I knew I was going to be a nun."

We walk quietly around the school to the chapel. St. Bernadette's for Girls is a rectangular, brick building, very schoolish. It is attached like an afterthought to the beautiful little stone chapel, which is the color of storm clouds.

I cross myself and say, "God's house."

"Hmmm?"

"That's what my parents told me when I was little. Church is God's house."

"Yes. That's a nice image, isn't it?"

I shrug. "I didn't know it was an image. I thought it was a fact."

"What did it make you think of, when they called it God's house?"

I look at the chapel. "Shelter. Safety." I think of

all the times I've been to Nat's house and Grace's house and even Cluck's house. "Friendship. Company." I think of the day I went to Curtis's house, how I wanted to be surrounded by where he lived. I think of how I used to sit on the curb, gawking at his bedroom window, and suddenly I have to hold back a huge giggle, because if Sister asked me what I was laughing about, how could I tell her that I was wondering if God keeps his underwear in church?

She smiles. "God's house is a good place to visit, you know, when everything is wrong."

The bell rings and I hand my latest poem to Sister Jude. I go to my next class thinking about God's house, boy problems, and the fact that a nun, who once wanted to be an actress, is turning out to be a pretty good friend.

chapter 17

Grace Boccaluzzo's house smells like Italian sausage—all the time, even if they're eating tuna fish. Curtis's house smelled like that soufflé his mother was making. Cluck's house smells clean and soapy, because there are six kids in his family and Mrs. McNally is always doing laundry. Sometimes I try to smell my house, after I've been out all day and I come back in. But I never can. And you just can't say to your friends, "Hey, your house smells like Italian sausage, how about mine?"

Grace and I went to her house directly from school, because today she is going to call Russell Blake to ask him to the spring formal and she is a nervous wreck. Grace is sitting cross-legged on her bed with the phone in her lap. And here's me, Little Miss Moral Support, telling her, "Go ahead. Call. He likes you."

"What if he's busy that night?"

"Then he's busy that night. But he won't be."

"Are you saying he's not popular, C.C.?"

I roll my eyes. "No, I am not saying he's not popular. I just have this feeling he won't be busy. Call."

"I wish it was Cluck."

"Forget Cluck. He's got a nymphet fetish. Call Russell, Grace. *Call*!"

She dials. She's petrified. "It's ringing."

"That's good."

She waits. He answers. Grace holds the receiver a little away from her ear so I can hear what he's saying. Russell goes, "What's new, Grace?"

"Nothing. What's new with you?"

"I accidentally threw away my retainer at lunch today, but the janitor let me dig through the garbage until I found it."

Russell Blake is quite the conversationalist.

Grace looks a little pale. "I was wondering, would you like to go to the St. Bernadette's spring formal with me? It's this Saturday."

I feel sorry for Grace. Her heart isn't in this, I

can tell. She's got it bad for Cluck. But Russell is a nice kid. And I can tell from the look of relief—not joy, but relief—that he said he'd go.

When she hangs up, Grace flies into her closet and starts this full-fledged panic about what she's going to wear. I wonder what Russell will think when he comes to her house to pick her up for the dance and smells sausage. Every time *I* walk into Grace's house, I feel as if I should order a pizza.

"What if Russell wants to kiss?" she asks. I guess she figures she's consulting an expert.

I shrug. "Do you want to kiss Russell?"

She is pulling a lacy, white dress over her head. (Natalie would say: You should step into it.) "I'd rather kiss Cluck."

"That is not an option."

"No, I don't want to kiss Russell."

"Then don't." That is the best advice I can give and I mean it sincerely.

The lacy, white number looks exactly like the dress I wore to make my First Holy Communion. Grace doesn't seem to realize this, so I break it to her gently.

"Take it off, Grace. Try something else."

She says she's going to try on her sister's green silk and goes across the hall to get it. While she's gone, I pick up the white dress and hold it against me in front of the mirror. A couple of snapshots flash through my mind: me in my veil with Grandma Carruthers, Cluck and me on the steps of the church, the big cake with the butter cream frosting and blue letters that said, "God Bless Cecily."

Finally, Grace reappears and says, "Well?"

I turn away from the mirror and almost drop the lace dress. "Mother of God."

Grace is wringing her hands. "Is that good or bad?"

"Grace, you look really, really, *really* nice." And she does. The green silk shows off Grace's figure, which is usually hidden under yards of puke-plaid.

Grace smiles, not certain, but hopeful.

"I mean it! And your hair looks great, too."

"You think?"

I nod enthusiastically. Grace always wears her dark hair pulled back in a long braid, but she's brushed it out and it falls down around her shoulders in waves. She looks like someone you'd see in a shampoo commercial.

Grace gets shy all of a sudden and says she'd better take the dress off before her sister comes home and strangles her with it. Then I say I have to go anyway, but I don't tell her the reason, which is that there's this poem I absolutely have to write.

I grab my book bag and leave. As soon as I am around the corner from Grace's house, I sit down on the curb and start scribbling in my English notebook like a maniac.

That's the thing about poetry—it can sneak up on you like a little kid with a squirt gun.

CONFESSION

I am a guest
In the house of my only hope,
My sins are lost
In the echo of footsteps.

In white lace
I sat trembling.
Today, they said,
I must swallow God
(I am too small for God
I will choke,
Choke on holiness.)
But we marched
Like solemn soldiers
To the altar to be blessed,

To shudder Amen,
And the wine was new
And warm on my lips.

At home I turned the gold cross
Over in my palm, hid in the corner,
 feeling unchanged.

The Madonna on my mother's table
Is carved, I pretend,
From white chocolate
Her hands are long and slim
But not to caress, to pray.
I am too afraid to understand.

He raises his hands
In a blessing like liquid
That rains like forgiveness
"And also with you."

In the silence of chapel
I slip from the kneeler
To the stone of the floor
To heal my unbelief.
I lower my eyes
And pray.

_____**chapter 18**

Patrick O'Connell is taking me to the formal.

Cluck is taking Kelly Sinclair, Grace Boccaluzzo is taking Russell Blake, and Natalie is going with Frankie Bruno. I am wearing a dress that belongs to Nat, which she wore to her cousin's wedding last summer. It's black linen, off-the-shoulder, and I love it.

I have not thought about Curtis Piperfield in days, so I am no longer his biggest fan. Fine with me.

St. Bernadette's gym is not exactly the classiest place, but what it lacks in elegance it makes up for in size. Kelly Sinclair headed up the decorations committee. It is clear, as she comes giggling in on Cluck's arm, that she decorated the gym to match her dress. The balloons and streamers and paper cups are the same obnoxious peachy color as her outfit. That's Kelly in a nutshell.

Natalie and Frankie come in right behind Cluck and Kelly. Natalie is wearing one of the dresses that didn't do a thing for me, but which looks very nice on her. I decide Frankie's nostrils are perfectly scaled to the rest of him, and I am happy that Nat looks so happy.

Patrick and I are officially an item now; Nat told me that Frankie told her that this news broke a lot of hearts at St. Simon Peter's Boys Prep. I am not bragging, I am repeating information obtained from a reliable source. There's a difference.

Cluck and Kelly find us and I can tell that Cluck is starting to get used to the idea of Pat and me. He seems to be enjoying Kelly, who *loves* my dress. She also loves my hair. She loves the way I've done my nails and the color of my lipstick, and I almost say: For crying out loud, Kelly, are you going to compliment me on how perfectly my ears are pierced?

For Cluck's sake, I don't say anything. Kelly must know that Cluck is still getting over his life-long crush on me, and she's going out of her way to show that she isn't jealous. Which she is.

Grace Boccaluzzo is as jealous of Kelly as Kelly is of me and I feel sorry for her. Russell has perfect teeth but he's no Gilbert McNally. Grace and Russell come off the dance floor and join our little huddle. Poor Grace. She looks miserable, watching Cluck parading Kelly the Nymphet around in front of the Preppies.

"Having fun, Grace?" I ask.

"Huh? Oh. Yeah." She is looking Kelly up and down. Talk about your impure thoughts. Grace looks as if she's plotting a slow and painful death for Kelly Sinclair. Maybe she'll strangle her with peach-colored streamers.

It hasn't sunk into Grace's head yet that she looks every bit as good as Kelly. I would even go so far as to say that tonight, she could qualify as a nymphet herself. I tell her again how great she looks, but old insecurities die hard. I shrug. She'll figure it out eventually.

The girls who are not drooling over Cluck are drooling over Patrick, and the ones who aren't drooling over Patrick are whispering about St. Simon Peter's lacrosse coach, the gorgeous Father Mike, who is one of the chaperones for the evening. I hope it's not a sin to think this, but Father Mike is extremely handsome. If he were a teacher at St.

B.'s, all the girls would take his class, even if he taught Intro to Eating Worms, that's how cute he is.

"C'mon, C.C.," Patrick says in that silky whisper, "let's dance."

He leads me out onto the dance floor and, unlike Frankie Bruno who is dancing with his hands almost on Natalie's behind, Patrick is a gentleman.

Lisa Bruno and her date are watching.

Walter Mert and his date (who plays girls' basketball at Miltondale) are watching.

Father Mike and Father Wink and all the nuns who teach at St. Bernadette's are watching.

The moon, caught dead center in one of the little windows near the gym's ceiling, appears to be watching.

And, of course, God is watching.

Thinking this makes me laugh.

"What's so funny?" Patrick asks.

"God is watching," I say, still giggling.

"Huh?"

"That's one of the first things they teach you in Catholic school," I explain, which, since Patrick O'Connell has been in Catholic school for as long as I have, he should know. "I wonder what He thinks."

"Who?"

"God."

Patrick grins. "He probably thinks that you should shut up so I can kiss you," he teases.

"It's not allowed," I remind him. But really, I'm wondering what God thinks. He probably thinks we worry too much. He probably isn't wild about rock and roll, like Bridget Glenn, and He probably would go out of His way to make sure a girl's house doesn't burn down so no one will ever get ahold of her personal journal. I'm also pretty sure God would never get mad at a little boy for daring another little boy to kiss a girl, even behind the baptismal font. Or for cussing. Or for thinking too much about kissing.

Along the perimeter of the basketball-court dance floor, the sisters are smiling, tapping their feet in their sensible shoes, drinking punch out of Kelly-colored cups. Sister Edward, Sister Marie Ignatius, Sister Jude, all of them.

They know.

They know that God is watching. They knew it, even before they heard it in the first grade at Our Lady of the Rosary, or St. Teresa's, or Christ the King, or Most Precious Blood Elementary. They knew it in their hearts. And all of a sudden, I like them. I like them because maybe once, a long time ago, they dreamed of getting married—to someone like Cluck or Patrick—in their school chapel. But then God said, "Wait a minute, before you do that, why don't you try working for me?"

And Father Wink, that frail little guy whose eye flutters, he knew, too. Maybe when he was a little boy in the suburbs of Rome working on his family's farm, maybe God sent an angel who said to Mario, "Don't worry about being small and skinny and having that nervous tic. So what if you'll never be a linebacker for Notre Dame? Don't worry, Mario! The Fighting Irish may not want you, but God does."

"What are you thinking?" Patrick asks, but I can't answer. I rest my face in that perfect spot below his collarbone and we dance close.

I'm thinking that I feel at home here in this gym, with the nuns and the priests and God watching. And I think I'm beginning to understand that the way I used to be Curtis Piperfield's biggest fan is pretty much the way the sisters and Father Wink feel about God.

It must sound insane to compare God to an eighth grader who originally wanted to be a rock star but then changed his mind and decided to be a certified public accountant. But the way I needed Curtis, the way I believed in him, the way he gave me a purpose, is the way the nuns feel about God.

The big difference, of course, is that Curtis is just a little twerp who likes big boobs.

And God . . .

. . . is God.

When the music stops, Patrick says he'd like to go say hello to Father Mike. Kelly is off talking to Lisa Bruno, and Russell has to go to the bathroom. I have no idea where Nat and Frankie are, so that leaves me and Grace Boccaluzzo and Cluck, who is staring at Grace as if he's never seen her before in his life.

And suddenly it hits her! The hair, the dress, the moon—she looks fabulous. And right before my eyes, Grace Boccaluzzo develops the single most important quality necessary to attract a delicious boy. Grace acquires confidence!

Cluck says, "Nice dress" (to Grace, not me).

Grace says, "Thank you. You look nice, too."

I happen to look really nice also, but neither of them mentions it. Then Grace says (to Cluck), "Kelly looks pretty, doesn't she?"

And Cluck—who has definitely brushed his hair tonight—says, "You look prettier" (to Grace, not me). And you know something? This does not bother me in the least little bit.

Honest.

─────────────chapter 19

Cluck knocks on my window at 12:15—in the afternoon. It's the day after the formal.

"Yow, C.C."

I climb out and we start walking. He doesn't have to tell me that he's just come from Sal Malanconico's father's barber shop; the shop is open from ten to noon every other Sunday, and Sal's friends get a pretty good discount.

Cluck's hair is not short, but it's neat and under control for the first time since I've known him.

Cluck says, "Let's go get some sodas, I'm thirsty as . . . I mean, I could really use a Coke."

We walk by Curtis Piperfield's house. We can see him through his bedroom window and he waves to us. He seems to be banging away on a calculator or something.

Cluck shakes his head. "Certified public accountant, huh?"

I nod. "That's what he said."

We talk about the dance for a while, how Kelly wound up talking to Lisa Bruno all night, how Patrick almost slugged some kid named Chip Wazalooski for asking me for my phone number, and how Natalie almost slugged Frankie Bruno for dancing with his hands on her rear end.

"It was a pretty fun night," Cluck says. "Um, I'm not in love with you anymore, C.C."

"That's good. It really is about time."

I start telling Cluck about the poems I've been writing and how Sister Jude thinks I've got talent and how maybe next year I'll take Sister Timothy's creative writing course, just for the heck of it. Then we walk for a long time without saying anything.

This, of course, is one of the best things about knowing someone since kindergarten—even a boy who's been in love with you until just last night. You can walk together without saying anything and it's okay.

We walk all the way to the center of town, past

Durgan's Pharmacy, past Braddock's, and when we get to the burger place, Cluck keeps walking, so I do, too.

Finally, I ask him, "Ever think about Catholic school?"

He looks at me as if I'm nuts. "Think about it?"

"Yeah. About going there and being Catholic on the outside but a teenager on the inside. And the nuns . . ."

"We've got priests. And brothers," he reminds me.

"Well, whoever . . . did you ever think about how they're so different than we are, but then again, not so different?"

"You're not going to read me one of your poems, are you, C.C.?"

I shrug. I don't know if he means right this instant or ever. Cluck thinks for a minute.

"You mean, like Father Mike?"

I nod.

Then he says, "At practice the other day, Bud Riley kept missing his hits. That's when you knock a guy out of the way to get the ball, C.C. So anyhow, Father Mike goes, 'Watch,' and he demonstrates on me. He sort of leaned into me and shoved and *wham*, I was down."

I smile. "That's exactly what I mean. Different, but not different."

We're quiet again and then I say, "Would you have loved me all along even if I always wrote poetry, even from the beginning?"

"C.C., I would have loved you if you had maggots in your hair and murdered kittens."

"Cluck!"

"C.C.! All I'm saying is, I would have loved you no matter what. I did love you no matter what."

"I'm sorry."

Cluck shakes his head hard. "Don't be. It felt good to love you. I'm just glad it's over."

And I know precisely how he feels.

We walk all the way past St. Bernadette's and I think, Sister Jude is there, reading Emily Dickinson. Father Wink is drinking espresso and going over the admissions applications for next year's freshman class. He is probably wearing one of his lucky hats.

And God is watching.

Cluck shoves his hands in his pockets and says, "Tell me about kissing."

I try not to smile. "Why? Still looking to kiss a nymphet?"

"Maybe."

We turn onto Grace Boccaluzzo's street and I smile because suddenly, I understand. My best friend Gilbert says very casually, but with a weird little tremble in his voice:

"Grace Boccaluzzo lives in that house."